Greetings, f

It's me, Carly! And this? Well, to explain that I need a little help. See, on our Web show, Sam has a remote that makes sound effects. I can't use it here so this is where you come in: When you see something in brackets, make that sound. Trust me on this — it's going to be great! So anyway, what is this? This is the next best thing to watching iCarly on the Web [drumroll, please] . . . this is the first iCarly book!!! [applause] Okay now, settle down, settle down.

Basically, you can consider these pages the first installment in the iHistory of iCarly. I know — how awesome is that, right? And it's not just about me, everyone's here! Sam [audience cheers], Freddie, my brother Spencer, Miss Briggs [audience boos] . . . even Lewbert [ewwww] . . . maybe I should have left him out. Oh well, it's all about having fun and keeping it real so settle back, grab your favorite smoothie, and get ready to laugh.

Remember: Keep watching iCarly — bye for now!

People of Earth

iHave a Web Show!

Adapted by Laurie McElroy

Part 1: Based on the episode "iPilot"
Written By Dan Schneider

Part 2: Based on the episode "iWant More Viewers"
Written By Steve Holland & Steven Molaro

Based on the TV Series *iCarly* Created By
Dan Schneider

SIMON AND SCHUSTER

SIMON AND SCHUSTER

First published in Great Britain in 2009 by Simon & Schuster UK Ltd,
1st Floor, 222 Gray's Inn Road, London WC1X 8HB
A CBS COMPANY

Originally published in the USA by Scholastic, 2009

© 2009 Viacom International Inc. All Rights Reserved.
Nickelodeon, Nickelodeon iCarly, and all related titles, logos and characters
are trademarks of Viacom International Inc.
All rights reserved, including the right to reproduce this book or
portions thereof in any form whatsoever

A CIP catalogue record for this book is available from the British Library

ISBN 978-1-84738-625-0

10 9 8 7 6 5 4 3 2 1

Printed by CPI Cox & Wyman, Reading, Berkshire RG1 8EX

www.simonandschuster.co.uk and www.nick.co.uk

iPilot

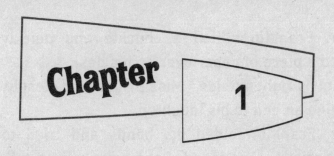

Chapter 1

Carly Shay nervously waited outside Principal Franklin's office. Her best friend Sam (short for Samantha) Puckett spent a lot of time with Mr. Franklin, the principal of Ridgeway School. Carly had met him before, of course, but she had never been called to his office for being in trouble. This was a new experience for her, and not one she was enjoying.

She anxiously ran her hand through her long, dark brown hair, and wondered for the tenth time in ten minutes how she had let Sam get her into this mess.

Behind the principal's closed door, Carly thought she heard laughter. She eyed her teacher, Miss Briggs, the reason she was here. Miss Briggs glared back at her, and then opened the door to the office.

Mr. Franklin stifled a chuckle and quickly turned a piece of paper over on his desk.

"She is right outside," Miss Briggs said sternly, bringing an end to his laughter.

Mr. Franklin folded his hands and tried to look serious. "Yes, good. Let's have a little talk with her."

"Carly, get in here right now," Miss Briggs demanded, snapping her fingers.

Carly entered the office.

"Have a seat," Mr. Franklin said.

Carly sat and looked around. Mr. Franklin's office was filled with pictures of the Ridgeway bulldog, the school mascot. A United States flag stood in the corner. Family pictures sat on the file cabinet behind his desk.

"So, I understand you put some flyers up all over the school," Mr. Franklin said.

Carly considered her answer for a moment. *Should I tell the truth?* she wondered. "Yes. I did," she admitted.

Miss Briggs stood behind the principal. When she heard Carly confess, the teacher looked like she wanted to leap across the room.

"Miss Briggs . . ." the principal warned.

The teacher took a deep breath. "I'm calm," she said.

"This flyer," the principal continued. He turned the paper over and started to laugh again. He tried to cover it with a cough, but it was obvious that he found the whole prank to be pretty funny. "It's a . . ."

Carly could feel herself starting to smile. The flyer was hilarious! But she quickly put on a serious face again.

"It's not funny!" Miss Briggs yelled at the principal. Then she turned to Carly. "Why would you photodoc my head onto the body of a rhinoceros?" she demanded.

"Well I —"

"Rhinoceros?" Mr. Franklin asked, showing Miss Briggs the flyer. "Oh no, she made you look like a hippopotamus."

"No. No. She's a rhinoceros," Carly said. "A hippo has fatter thighs and a wider snout."

Mr. Franklin looked at the picture again. "I thought rhinos had the fat thighs."

"No," Carly explained. "If you see a picture of the two of them together you can really —"

Miss Briggs cut them off with a snarl. "What does it matter?" she yelled.

Carly and Mr. Franklin both sat back, their hippo vs. rhino discussion brought to an end.

"I think we should call her father in to discuss this," Miss Briggs demanded.

"Uh, my dad's stationed in Europe right now," Carly told her. Actually, her father was stationed on a submarine. So technically, he was *under* Europe — or Europe's waters. Carly wasn't quite sure exactly where he was. She missed him, of course, but she was happy to stay behind in Seattle.

"He's in the military," Mr. Franklin added.

"Well, there must be some adult in charge of her," Miss Briggs said.

"My older brother, Spencer," Carly said.

Miss Briggs remembered him. Carly's brother, Spencer, had also been a student at Ridgeway. "Oh yes," she drawled sarcastically. "The artist."

Miss Briggs's scorn was clear from her tone of

voice, but Carly defended her brother. "He's a great artist!"

"Look, we don't need to call her brother in about this," Mr. Franklin said. "I'm sure you can come up with a suitable punishment."

Miss Briggs thought about it for a moment. Then her eyes lit up and her face broke into a nasty grin. "Fine," she said with a wicked chuckle. "You know, Carly, I am in charge of the talent show this year."

"Yeah," Carly nodded. "You're holding auditions on Saturday."

"No. You are," Miss Briggs answered.

"Huh?" Carly asked. Watching lame talent show auditions was the last thing she wanted to do with her weekend.

"I will be enjoying my Saturday while you videotape the auditions for me." Miss Briggs handed over a list of students who had signed up to try out for the show.

Carly glanced at it. It was a long list. It would take all day on Saturday to get through that many auditions. She jumped to her feet and turned to

7

Principal Franklin for support. "No! I'm going to see Cuddle Fish play live at the Hawthorne on Saturday!"

"Not anymore," Miss Briggs said in a singsong voice. Clearly, the idea of making Carly miss the concert brought her more joy than anything else had in a long, long time.

"Aw, c'mon..." Carly pleaded, glancing at Principal Franklin again.

But Miss Briggs was not about to back down. "That's what you get for turning me into a hippopotamus."

"Rhinoceros," Carly said, correcting her and trying not to grin when Principal Franklin snorted with laughter.

Miss Briggs was so angry she practically breathed fire. "Get out!" she said fiercely, pointing at the door.

"Right." Carly opened the door and ran. She wanted to get away before Miss Briggs could think of any more mean and nasty punishments.

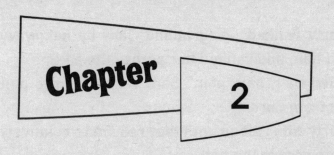

Chapter 2

Carly found Sam by her locker. As usual, Sam was torturing someone. She had a classmate named Rico pinned up against the row of lockers.

"Owwww! Lemme go!" Rico yelled.

"Say you're sorry," Sam insisted.

Rico caved. "I'm sorry!"

But Sam wasn't quite finished. She tightened her grip on Rico's shirt. "And what are you sorry for?" she asked sweetly.

"For saying that you're aggressive," Rico whimpered.

"And what am I again?" Sam asked him with a fierce look.

"Pretty and sweet," Rico said.

"Thank you," Sam said, in a voice that was anything but pretty and sweet. "Now the next time I —"

Carly walked up, grabbed Sam by her wavy blond hair, and yanked her across the hall.

"Ow! Hair, hair, hair," Sam said, trying to pull away from Carly.

Carly didn't let go until they reached a relatively private spot in the hall.

"Hi," Carly said in an angry tone of voice. Her brown eyes flashed.

"Did you get in trouble?" Sam asked.

"Of course I got in trouble! Teachers tend to get upset when you put their heads on the bodies of big, fat animals!" Carly yelled. "I can't believe I let you talk me into taking the blame for you!"

"You had to," Sam reasoned, throwing her arms up into the air. "I've already been suspended once this semester. If I'd gotten busted, they'd have expelled me!"

"Well here's an idea," Carly said sweetly.

"What?"

She put her face inches from Sam's and yelled, "Stop doing bad things!"

Carly loved the fact that Sam was crazy and unpredictable, not to mention a totally loyal friend. But helping Sam stay out of trouble could

10

be exhausting. And this time, keeping Sam out of trouble meant that Carly's entire Saturday was ruined. Correction — Carly and Sam's entire Saturday was ruined. There was no way she was going to watch all those auditions alone.

Sam rolled her eyes. It wasn't a bad thing. It was funny. The whole school cracked up when they saw those flyers. And who hadn't ever looked at Miss Briggs and thought, *She looks like a rhinoceros?*

Sam loved her best friend. Carly was funny and mature and loveable. But she got way too stressed about the small things. "*Okaaaay,*" Sam drawled. "Chillax."

Carly pushed past Sam and walked over to her locker. "I will not chillax," she said sarcastically. "And get excited, because you and I get to spend our entire Saturday here videotaping kids' auditions for the talent show."

"No way! Gross!" Sam moaned.

"Sorry, that's my punishment. So now it's your punishment too," Carly said. Her tone of voice made it clear — there was no way Sam was getting out of this one.

"Whatev," Sam said with a shrug.

Carly grabbed a book from her locker and then slammed it shut. "You know, anybody but me would punch you right in the head."

Sam smiled sweetly. "Which is why you are my best friend."

"Good to know. Now why are you mine?" Carly turned on her heel and walked toward her class.

Sam ran after her, pushing Rico into his locker as she passed him. "Because I'm a loveable person," she said.

Carly headed straight home after school, still disappointed that her plans to see Cuddle Fish on Saturday were ruined. She got off the elevator in her high-rise building and headed for the loft she shared with her older brother Spencer. They lived in a cool, old industrial building in downtown Seattle that had been converted to apartments and artist lofts.

Carly slipped her key into the lock and dropped her water bottle.

The door across the hall flew open and her neighbor, Freddie, burst into the hall. He grabbed the bottle and jumped up to hand it to Carly before she could even think about bending down to get it herself.

"You dropped this," Freddie said with a grin.

Freddie was also in the eighth grade at Ridgeway. Carly liked him — as a friend. However, Freddie had been crushing on her ever since she could remember, and sometimes it got a little embarrassing for Carly. Like now.

"Um, thanks, but you really —"

"I was going to walk you home from school, but I couldn't find you," Freddie interrupted. He was over-the-top with excitement just to be standing in the hall with her. "So hey!" he said, giving her a little wave.

"Freddie, were you just looking out your peephole, waiting for me to come home?" Carly asked.

"No-ho-ho," Freddie said with a laugh.

But Carly knew he wasn't telling the truth. "Freddie . . ."

"Yes," he admitted.

Carly sighed. She had told Freddie a hundred times that she just wanted to be friends. "I thought we talked about this. We can be buds, but you've got to get over this crush thing," she said sweetly.

"I am over it. Seriously," Freddie insisted. "I'm in love with you. You just want to be friends. And I'm totally cool living with that constant pain," he explained.

Carly rolled her eyes and laughed.

"Hey, I hear you need to borrow a camcorder to tape some auditions," Freddie said.

"Yeah, but I'll just use my brother's," Carly said.

"Well, if you change your mind, you know my digits." Freddie pulled his phone out of his pocket and showed it to her. He was a total techno geek, and always had the latest equipment, from phones to cameras to computers.

"Hey, you got a new cell phone," Carly said.

Freddie shoved it toward her. "You can have it!"

Carly shook her head and opened the door to her loft, making sure that Freddie stayed in the hall.

14

"I'm home," she called.

"Hey, kiddo!" her brother Spencer said.

Carly looked around, trying to figure out where Spencer's voice was coming from.

"Up here," he said, waving from his perch on a ceiling rafter. "Just taking some pics of my robot."

Carly thought her brother was a brilliant sculptor, and half the fun of living with him was coming home to discover what Spencer had created while she was out. Today there was a giant statue of a robot, made out of plastic bottles. Carly looked at the robot's red eyes, then up at her brother.

"Smile!" Spencer said, snapping a couple of photos.

"You know, for most eighth-grade girls, if they came home and found their twenty-six-year-old brother dangling upside down from the ceiling over a giant robot made out of soda bottles . . . it'd be weird," Carly joked.

Spencer seemed to think about this for a moment. "You're saying I'm abnormal," he said in a serious tone of voice.

Carly laughed. Abnormal? Spencer was goofy and eccentric — offbeat even — but he was always

there when Carly needed him. Ultimately, he was a responsible guardian.

"Do I need to say it?" she asked. "Come down from there before you hurt yourself."

"No worries," Spencer told her. "I've got my leg wrapped around this pipe —"

But Spencer spoke too soon. At that moment he slipped and dropped like a rock, hitting the floor with a giant thud.

"I can't believe you're in charge of me," Carly said with a laugh. Sometimes she wondered who was really the grown-up.

"Please help me stand up," Spencer groaned.

Carly helped him to his feet. "Are you all right?" she asked.

Spencer started to say yes, then grabbed his shoulder. "Nope. I dislocated my shoulder again." He rolled his shoulder back, then forward. It didn't click into place. "One sec . . ."

Spencer jumped into the air and threw himself onto the floor again. There was a yell, followed by a loud crunching sound. "Yeah, that fixed her," Spencer said, jumping to his feet.

"Good. So listen, I need a favor," Carly said.

16

"Shoot," Spencer said.

"I have to tape a bunch of auditions at school on Saturday," Carly explained.

"Fun," Spencer said.

"Yeah, not really," Carly told him. "Anyway, would you let me borrow your video camera?"

"I would," Spencer said.

"Awesome."

"Though, I can't," Spencer said slowly.

"Why not?" Carly asked, confused.

Spencer laughed and reached behind him with a sheepish expression. "I made it into a squirrel," he admitted. He showed her the video camera, which now looked like the body of a squirrel. A small Nerf football had been attached to make a head, and there was a long, orange tail trailing behind.

Carly shook her head with a laugh. Life with Spencer was never boring.

17

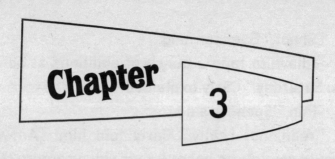
Saturday morning, Carly entered the school auditorium. Sam was on her cell phone, claiming to be trapped outside and unable to get into the school.

"I told you the front door would be locked," Carly said into her cell phone. "You've got to go around to the blue doors in back of the —" She stopped short when she got a look at the camera equipment Freddie had set up. It looked like he was getting ready to film a Hollywood blockbuster, not some school talent show auditions. "Oh my gosh!"

"Morning, Carly!" Freddie said happily.

"See you in a sec," Carly said, closing her phone. "Freddie!"

Freddie flashed a proud grin. "What do you think of my equipment?" he asked.

Carly was more than a little overwhelmed. Freddie had gone completely over the top, as usual. "I just asked to borrow your video camera. What is all this?" she asked.

Freddie pointed to his camera and launched into techno-geek speak. "Well, that's a three-chip-high camcorder with a hyper-cardioid condenser microphone mounted on a carbon fiber tripod with a low-drag fluid head."

Carly had no idea what he was talking about.

Then Freddie picked up a tray from the table. "I also brought you juice and a bagel," he said happily. A bud vase with a daisy in it sat next to the plate, and Carly noticed that he had brought her favorite brand of cream cheese.

Sam strolled through the auditorium doors, sipping a cup of coffee. "Hey, you invited the doof," she said when she spotted Freddie.

"Sam," Carly scolded. She knew Sam didn't like Freddie, but he was doing them a favor.

Freddie slammed the tray back on the table. He didn't like Sam any more than she liked him. "Aw, man! I didn't know THAT was gonna be here," he said, pointing to Sam.

"She. I'm a she, Freddie — as in girl," Sam said sarcastically.

"Barely," Freddie muttered.

Sam pretended to be scared of him. "Ooooooh."

"You just keep your hands off my AV equipment," Freddie warned her.

"You mean I can't play with the balance on your super-dee-duper-dee camcorder?" Sam teased.

"Ah, sure," Freddie yelled, throwing his arms up into the air. "Everybody jokes about the balance till the skin tones go magenta!"

Sam cleared her throat. She knew exactly how to push Freddie's buttons, and there was nothing she enjoyed more. "Bet you'd let Carly..." she said in a singsong voice.

"That's it!" Freddie yelled, slamming the table. He was totally fed up. "I'm taking my stuff and I'm going home!" He picked up his camcorder.

Sam wasn't the only one who knew how to get a reaction out of Freddie. Sam knew how to make him crazy-mad. Carly knew how to draw the

opposite reaction. She moved in front of Sam and flashed a sweet smile at Freddie. "Please stay," she said.

Freddie melted instantly. "Okay," he agreed. He smiled back at Carly, and then glared at Sam.

Carly realized she would be doing more than watching auditions all day — she'd also be watching Freddie and Sam, making sure they didn't hurt each other.

A few minutes later, Carly called in the first guy who had signed up to audition. She and Sam sat behind a table, ready to take notes, while Freddie videotaped.

"Okay, Jeb, you ready to audition?" Carly asked.

Jeb took the stage. He wore a black beret, a black shirt, and black jeans with red suspenders. "Yeah. I'll be performing a scene from a French play called, *La Ou Est Ma Femme.*"

"*Okaaay,*" Sam said slowly. *Was this guy actually going to do the scene in French?* she wondered. Because she didn't speak that language.

"We don't know what that means," she admitted. "But knock us out."

Carly turned to Freddie. "Rolling?"

Freddie turned on the camera. "Rolling . . ."

Jeb started to speak in a bad French accent, gesturing wildly with his arms. "But . . . but where did she go?" he asked.

The actor played both characters in his scene, answering himself by holding up a fake mustache on the end of a stick, and trying to deepen his voice. "I don't know." He used the same bad French accent.

"But when will she be back?" he asked, dropping the mustache.

Mustache-man answered, "I don't know!"

"Well, where can I find her?" Jeb asked.

He held up the fake mustache and pretended to be angry. "I tell you, I do not know!" he insisted.

Carly eyed Sam, wishing one of Jeb's characters would find the mystery woman already.

Sam was secretly hoping the two characters would get into a fistfight so she could watch Jeb punch himself in the nose.

But Jeb brought his scene to an end instead. He stayed onstage waiting for a reaction. He had a huge smile on his face, so clearly he thought he had done a good job.

"Okay!" Carly said with a smile.

"Nice job!" Sam added.

Satisfied, Jeb bowed and left the stage.

"What'd ya think?" Sam asked.

Carly imitated Jeb's bad accent. "I don't know!"

Sam did the same. "You don't know?"

"I tell you, I do not know," Carly said, trying to sound like a French man.

"But you must know!" Sam insisted, sounding equally manly and equally French — in other words, not at all manly and not at all French.

"How can I know when I do not know?" Carly asked.

"I don't know," Sam answered.

Freddie stood behind the camera and laughed. Filming the girls' reactions to Jeb's performance was way more fun than filming Jeb.

By the tenth audition — a girl playing a totally

boring song badly on the cello — Sam turned to Carly to find her friend fast asleep.

She didn't stay asleep long. Soon they were all wide awake, pinned to their chairs in horror while a perfectly normal-looking classmate made a complete and total fool out of himself trying to dance ballet. Wearing black tights and a bright yellow, frilly shirt, Jason Hughes slipped and teetered and tottered around onstage. He made himself dizzy with his twirls, and Carly and Sam nauseous with his pliés. Even Freddie was shocked by the awfulness of it all.

By the time Taryn James came in with her trumpet, the girls were doing their best to stay awake.

"I will play the trumpet," Taryn said.

"Great," Carly said, not even pretending to be interested.

"Nice," Sam muttered, wishing she had thought to bring earplugs with her.

". . . while hopping on this pogo stick," Taryn added.

Carly and Sam turned to each other with a

24

smile. Finally! Something weird and fun and freaky! An act kids would actually want to watch onstage.

Freddie perked up and looked through the camera lens.

Taryn started hopping on the pogo stick, and then brought the trumpet to her lips and began to blow. She was one of the funniest acts they had seen that day.

Sam and Carly gave her a standing ovation. "That's what I'm talking 'bout!" Carly said happily.

"Great job!" Sam added.

"You go, girl!" Carly shouted.

Sam applauded some more. "Yeah, pogotastic!"

Carly and Sam enjoyed Taryn and her pogo/trumpet act so much that they were hopeful for the rest of the auditions, but the very next act was a red-haired boy named Myron. He announced he would be doing stand-up comedy.

Carly was so bored by the first half of his very long and tiresome joke that her mind drifted off

to something more fun, like having a tooth filled, or taking an incredibly hard history test. Then she realized that Myron was finally getting to the punch line.

"So the doc says, 'Why'd you wait so long to bring her in?'" Myron said. "So I say, 'I liked the eggs.'" Myron cracked himself up. He doubled over with laughter.

Carly and Sam looked at each other. Was this the part where they were supposed to laugh? They forced out a chuckle or two.

"Thanks!" Myron said, laughing himself off stage.

"Not that funny," Carly said, as soon as he was out of earshot.

"No, no, not at all," Sam agreed, getting up and walking across the room. She faced Carly from the stage. "But forget that. Can we please discuss the boy's hair and glasses? He looks like Miss Briggs."

Carly laughed. "Yeah, except he doesn't have Miss Briggs's crazy pointy ears."

Freddie focused his camera on the girls. Their comedy routine was a lot funnier than Myron's.

Sam didn't realize she was on camera. "I know," she said, agreeing with Carly. "What is up with those?"

"It's like she stuffs waffle cones on them to make them pointier," Carly said, laughing.

"Totally! I mean she could poke an eye out with one of those things." Sam tilted her head sideways, pretending to be ready to poke Carly's eye out.

The girls cracked up. Freddie did, too.

"Okay, okay, we better keep going," Carly said when she stopped giggling. She checked her audition list. "We've still got eleven more kids to see."

Sam threw her head back and howled. "Nooooo! Eleven!"

"Calm down," Carly told her. "They can't get worse."

But Carly spoke too soon.

By the end of the afternoon, all the girls could do was sit and stare in stunned horror while a boy used his mouth and a microphone to sound like a drum. Beatboxing could be fun to listen to as part of a hip-hop song, but that was all this guy had.

There was no music. No lyrics. No dancing. Just a guy sputtering into a microphone for an insanely long time. Bad sounds. Bad, bad sounds.

". . . and I was wrong," Carly admitted. Things could get worse. They could get much, much worse. And they had.

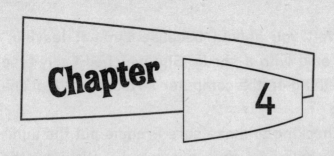

Chapter 4

That night, Carly and Sam sprawled out on the sofa in front of the television. They forgot all about the bad auditions and lost themselves in a movie. The next thing Carly knew, she was waking up. Sam was asleep on the other end of the sofa.

"Sam, Sam, wake up ..." Carly said, giving Sam's cheek a nudge with her bare foot.

Sam yawned. "What time is it?" she asked.

"Late," Carly said, sitting up. "What time is your mom coming to pick you up?"

"She's not," Sam answered, reaching for a bottle of water. "I told her you invited me to spend the night."

Carly look confused. "I didn't invite you to spend the night." She walked over to the computer that she kept on the kitchen island. She liked to do her homework in the center of things.

"Well you should because I'm not leaving," Sam said with a shrug. She watched Carly type something on the computer keyboard. "What'cha doing?"

"Checking to make sure Freddie put the auditions online," she answered, clicking the mouse. "I told Miss Briggs we'd upload them on SplashFace tonight so she could watch them in the morning."

Sam yawned again, and then stood up to stretch. Sleeping on the couch had left her stiff. "I kinda hate Miss Briggs. Remember when she called me a demon?"

Carly was focused on the computer screen. She found the SplashFace site and then clicked around until she found the right page. Suddenly her brown eyes widened and she screamed. "No!"

"Oh yeah," Sam said. "It was when I put that raw chicken in her purse and she —"

But that wasn't what made Carly scream. It was something worse — much, much worse. "Be quiet and come look at this!" she said, her voice rising in panic.

30

Sam walked over to Carly and looked over her shoulder. "What, Freddie didn't upload the auditions?"

Carly was completely and totally horrified. "No — he uploaded us!"

Now it was Sam's turn to scream. "What?"

"Look!" Carly said, pointing to the computer screen.

Sam stood next to her and stared at the screen in horror. It was a video clip of the two of them, making fun of Jeb and his totally bad French accent. "That's you and me!" Sam said, stating the obvious.

"Sure is!" Carly answered.

Sam's eyes narrowed at the memory of Freddie standing behind them with all his camera equipment. He had totally invaded their privacy! "He wasn't supposed to film us! We were being all goofy and acting like idiots all day!"

As the video continued to play, Carly remembered someone else they had made fun of that day. "Oh my gosh, we made fun of Miss Briggs and her crazy pointy ears!"

"Whoa, if she sees that..." Sam said,

31

imagining the various ways Miss Briggs could get back at them.

"*Anyone* can see it!" Carly said. She was in full panic mode. "It's on SplashFace!"

Sam took a deep breath and tried to calm down. "Okay, okay, chillax," she said, as much for her own benefit as for Carly's. "Look," she said, pointing at the computer screen. "See the view count? Only twenty-seven people have clicked on it."

"Oh. Okay, good," Carly said, relaxing for a second. She took another look at the screen. Her panic level started to rise again. "Sam?"

"Yeah?"

"That's twenty-seven thousand!!!" Carly screamed.

Her scream was so loud that she blew Sam off the chair and onto the floor. Carly stared at the screen in complete and total shock. Once Miss Briggs got a look at that video, life as they knew it was over. Completely and totally over. Miss Briggs would find all kinds of evil ways to get back at them. They'd never have a free Saturday again.

Carly took some deep breaths and tried to get her heart to stop beating so fast. Once she had a

minute to calm down, she realized that if Freddie could post the video, she could try to unpost it. She worked her way through SplashFace, going from menu to menu, and typing as fast as she could, to take the video off-line.

Sam paced behind her. "Can you remove it?" she asked.

"Maybe," Carly said, clicking the mouse. But she had reached a dead end. "Ugh! I need Freddie's password."

"Which apartment does he live in?" Sam asked.

"The one across the hall." Carly checked the clock on the computer. "But it's after midnight so you probably shouldn't —"

But Sam was already gone. If getting Freddie out of bed at midnight was what it took to get that video off of SplashFace, that's what she'd do.

Carly kept typing, focused on the screen. A bell rang on the SplashFace page. "Oh great," she moaned. "Now twenty-*eight* thousand people have watched us."

The next thing Carly heard was Freddie screaming. She turned around to see Sam

33

dragging him across the hall in his red pajamas. He was on his back, being yanked through the door by his foot.

"Quit it, Sam! Let go of my foot!" he yelled. "Too much friction! Let go!"

Sam let go and Freddie scrambled to his feet.

"What is the matter with you?" Freddie asked. Not only was he embarrassed to be dragged out of bed by a girl. Now he was standing in front of Carly, his crush, wearing his dorky pajamas.

Carly was too freaked to notice. "Why did you film us at the auditions today?" she asked.

"Oh, because you guys were being funny," Freddie answered.

"Well, you shouldn't have put us online without our permission!" Sam said.

"I didn't! I edited you guys out before I uploaded the auditions," Freddie explained.

"No, you did the opposite of that!" Carly told him.

"What?" Freddie started typing on Carly's computer. He knew he had edited the girls out of the video footage. He was sure of it. "There's no way I —"

34

Freddie stopped protesting when he saw Carly and Sam laughing behind the audition table. He had screwed up — big time. "Uh-oh."

"Yeah," Sam agreed.

"Just take us off the site!" Carly begged. She was determined to get that video off SplashFace before Miss Briggs logged on.

Freddie started typing. "Okay, okay! Just give me a sec. . . ."

"Ohhhh, this is so not good," Carly moaned. She paced back and forth, worrying. "Anyone . . . anyone in the world can just click and see everything we did and said today."

"It's so embarrassing," Sam agreed. "And if Miss Briggs sees —"

"Don't even talk about it," Carly said, cutting her off. "Because if she —"

"Ha! Got it!" Freddie said, clicking the mouse one last time. He read the computer screen. "See, it says, at your request, this video will be removed."

"Good!" Carly said, throwing her had back in relief.

"Finally," Sam said.

35

But Freddie hadn't finished reading the screen. "Tomorrow morning," he finished quietly.

"Aw, man!" Sam yelled.

"Freddie! Do you know how many more thousands of people can view it by then?" Carly asked desperately.

Freddie tried to salvage the situation. "All right, look, before you get all freaked out" — he clicked the mouse, looking for some good news — "SplashFace has message boards."

"So?" Sam asked.

"So, let's see what people are saying about the video." He clicked a few keys and opened the comments section of the message board. "Uhhh . . . okay, here's one: 'Carly, you and your friend Sam crack me up. Funny stuff.'"

"Great," Carly said. "So one kid thinks —"

"Wait," Freddie said. "SlackerBoy314 writes: 'Carly, you're pretty.'" He turned to look at her. "It's true," he said.

Sam nodded in agreement. "You are," she said.

"Stop," Carly said, beginning to feel a little embarrassed.

"Oh wait, check this one," Freddie said. "'Yo, Carly and Sam, you chicks are hilarious. When's your next show?'"

The girls looked at each other and smiled. The kids on SplashFace thought they were funny! That was kind of cool.

Freddie kept reading. "And this kid says: 'You guys are way better than most of the usual stuff here on SplashFace.'"

"Wow. They love us," Sam said.

"Yeah," Carly agreed.

But she was still worried. There was no way Miss Briggs would love them — even more than the usual stuff. What if she saw the video before the next morning?

Chapter 5

Monday morning at school, Carly and Sam waited for Miss Briggs in the hall outside the teacher's lounge.

Carly nervously checked the time on her cell phone, and paced up and down the hall. "Where's Miss Briggs?" she asked Sam. "What if she saw it?"

Sam tried to calm her friend down. "The video was off by yesterday morning," she assured her.

"What if she saw it before it was off?" Carly asked. The panic was rising in her voice again.

Sam hoped for the best. After all, why would Miss Briggs work on the weekend if she didn't have to? "It was the weekend," Sam said. "She was probably out having fun."

Carly doubted it. She couldn't see Miss Briggs having fun — at any time!

Sam spotted the teacher walking down the hall and tried to read her face. But Miss Briggs wore her usual expression — pinched and sour, like she had just sucked on a lemon.

Sam nudged Carly to let her know Miss Briggs was on her way. "Shhh, shhh!"

As soon as Miss Briggs spotted the girls, she broke into a big grin. "Hello, Carly. Samantha," she said pleasantly.

Carly breathed a sigh of relief. "Morning, Miss Briggs."

"Howdy," Sam said, equally relieved.

Carly handed the teacher a disc. "Um, we had some trouble putting the video online, so here's a DVD of every kid who auditioned on Saturday."

"Thank you," Miss Briggs said.

"Sure," Carly said uneasily.

Miss Briggs took the disc, and her tone changed. "I'll try not to poke a hole in this with my pointy ears," she said coldly.

Carly and Sam exchanged glances. They should have known something was wrong the minute

39

Miss Briggs acted nice. Miss Briggs was never nice. To anyone. Especially them.

"She saw the video," Sam said, stating the obvious.

"We're so sorry," Carly said to Miss Briggs.

"Yes, and I imagine you'll even be sorrier after I grade your next exams." Miss Briggs shook her head and started to walk away.

Carly had done some extra work, just in case Miss Briggs saw the video. Now was the time to hand it over. "Uh, Miss Briggs?" Carly said.

Miss Briggs turned around "What?" she demanded.

Carly held out a piece of paper. Maybe Miss Briggs would be a little less mad if she didn't have to watch all the auditions. "I typed up a list of the kids we think should be in the talent show," she said.

Miss Briggs snatched the paper from Carly's hand and looked at it with a sour expression. "Snorting milk? Pogo-stick hopping?" she scoffed. "These aren't talents."

"They were the most fun kids to watch," Sam explained.

"Pfft," Miss Briggs sneered. She handed the list back to Carly and waved her hand dismissively. "Good-bye."

"Wait," Carly said, "so you're not going to let any of the kids we picked be in the show?"

"That's right, girls." Miss Briggs flashed her evil grin and slammed her classroom door in their faces. She would choose who was going to be in the talent show herself. Nice acts like Jason Hughes doing ballet and cello players would make the cut, not the ridiculous acts Carly and Sam liked.

Somehow, Saturday's beatboxer hadn't gotten the word that Carly and Sam weren't exactly in charge of the talent show. He followed the girls down the hall, sputtering into his microphone.

Carly was already way too stressed to deal with one more thing. "No one enjoys that!" she yelled.

Carly was still steamed about Miss Briggs when she got home from school. She walked into

the apartment and threw her backpack on the couch. "I am so mad!" she said.

Sam was right behind her. "Me too," she agreed. "I need some ham." Sam was definitely a carnivore. Whenever anything went wrong, she ate — and meat was her favorite thing. Today was no exception. She headed for the refrigerator.

"Seriously, Miss Briggs is the worst!" Carly complained.

Sam was as at home in Carly's loft as she was in her own house. She grabbed the leftover ham from the refrigerator and looked for a carving knife. "You don't have to convince me. I disliked her even after she got that brown lump removed from her nose." She shuddered, remembering that horrible brown thing. It was huge.

There was a knock on the door. Carly walked across the room. "I'll tell you something," she said, checking the peephole and opening the door. "She is what's wrong with the world."

Freddie walked in. "Who's what's wrong with the world?" he asked.

"Miss Briggs," Carly answered.

"Oh," Freddie said, following Carly to the kitchen. "Well, hey, at least she got that brown lump taken off her nose."

Carly shook her head. "I just dislike it when adults like her get to control what kids can do and see. It bothers me."

Sam was only half listening. She was completely involved in slicing the ham. "Why do they put a bone right in the middle of a ham?" she asked.

Carly got a pitcher of juice out of the refrigerator. "Hey, remember all that stuff those kids wrote about us on the message boards?" Carly asked. The messages, combined with Miss Briggs's lame judgment when it came to talent, had given her an idea.

"Yeah," Sam said, popping a piece of ham into her mouth.

"Things like, 'You guys should upload more videos,' and, 'When's your next show?' and, 'We want more.'" Carly waited a moment to let the comments sink in. "Let's give them more," she announced.

43

"More?" Freddie asked.

"Okay, what are we talking about here?" Sam asked.

"Doing a Web show," Carly said, working out the details in her mind as she talked. "Online. Every week."

"Why?" Sam asked.

"Because it can be whatever we want it to be," Carly explained. The idea seemed better and better the more she thought about it. "No adults to say, 'You can do this — you can't do that.' We can do whatever we want, say whatever we want . . ."

Sam could see Carly was excited about the idea, and it sounded pretty cool. It also sounded like it would take a lot of time and effort, something Sam wasn't so good at. "Would it mean I have to do, like, work and stuff?" she asked, making a face as she said the word work.

"Well, if you're going to do a show you've got to prepare for it," Carly said.

"Eh, then make it your show," Sam said, popping another piece of ham into her mouth. "You do the work, I'll just show up and be your amusing little sidekick."

44

Freddie grabbed a piece of ham. "Wait, what's the show gonna be about?" he asked.

Carly shrugged. That was the beauty of it. It could be about whatever they wanted. "Anything. Something different every week." Then she got a brilliant idea. "But for the first show? Kids With Bizarro Talents," she announced.

She knew that doing a show of all those kids Miss Briggs dismissed would be a huge hit. Their classmates didn't want to see cello players and ballet dancers. They wanted to see crazy, wacky talents. It was the perfect way to start their new show.

"Ahhhh, clever," Sam said. "Miss Briggs says, 'No, no, no.' We say, 'Yeah, yeah, yeah.'"

"Hey, why don't you call your show *iCarly*," Freddie said. "You know, *I* — Internet. *Carly* — you."

"I like it," Sam said.

Carly agreed. "*iCarly*'s cool."

Freddie realized the show was an excellent opportunity to spend more time with Carly, even if that meant putting up with Sam. "And, um, you're going to need a technical producer, right?" he

asked. "To set up the lights, audio, work the camera?"

"Awww," Sam teased. "He wants to be our assistant. This could be fun. . . ."

Carly shook her head at Sam. Her friend was way too hard on Freddie.

"You've got a big mouth, lady," Freddie yelled at Sam.

"Is that a new shirt?" Sam asked, pointing at Freddie's yellow polo shirt. "I don't like it."

"I don't have to take that," Freddie said.

But Sam knew that he did. Because she was Carly's best friend. If Freddie wanted to hang with Carly, he had to put up with Sam, too. "Yeah you do," she said.

"All right," Freddie said, marching over to the kitchen island. "I am so —"

"Wah, wah, wah," Sam said, imitating his tone. "Wah, wah, wah."

"Oh, that is *soooo* mature," Freddie said.

But Sam didn't stop. "Wah, wah, wah," she said.

Freddie stooped to her level. "Blah, blah, blah, blah, blah," he said.

46

"Children . . ." Carly said. "Children . . ."

But her friends were too busy irritating each other to listen to her. She could see that she'd have to play peacemaker to make this Web show work. But right now, she didn't have the energy. She joined in, making as much nonsense noise as the rest of them.

They stopped only when Spencer ran in, carrying a ratty old mannequin. She was in two pieces. Her blond hair was dirty and tangled. And there was a hole in her left shoulder.

"Hey! Look what someone just left in a Dumpster," Spencer said. "Isn't she amazing?"

Carly was too caught up in the idea of her Web show to notice whether the mannequin was amazing or not. She ran up to her brother, followed by Sam and Freddie. She had the perfect place to film their Web show — the third floor of their loft. It was a big open space. They could fix it up and make it look really cool. There was plenty of room for all of Freddie's high-tech equipment, and Spencer's sculptures would make awesome props. An old industrial elevator off the kitchen could carry

them upstairs when they didn't feel like taking the stairs.

"Hey, can we use the third floor as kind of a TV studio?" she asked.

"I don't know," Spencer answered. "It depends on —"

Carly didn't really listen to his answer. Spencer always said yes, as long as whatever she wanted wasn't dangerous.

"Thanks!" she squealed, then ran up the stairs.

Sam was right behind her. "You rock!" she yelled over her shoulder.

Spencer watched them go, more than a little confused. "Wait, I didn't say . . . why do you . . ."

"Later!" Freddie yelled, following the girls.

"Okay, later," Spencer said. He was still wondering just exactly who it was he had said okay to, but he looked down at his mannequin and forgot all about Carly and her friends. It was time to make some art!

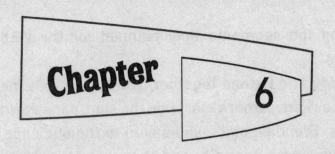

Chapter 6

A few days later, Carly, Sam, and Freddie were ready for their first live Web show. Carly ran out of her bedroom and into the kitchen. She grabbed a bottle of water from the refrigerator.

Freddie called down at her from upstairs. "Fifty-two seconds."

Carly punched the elevator button. It would be faster than taking the stairs. "Sam, come on!" she yelled. Sam ran up just as the elevator doors opened.

Freddie was watching the clock upstairs. "Forty-five seconds!"

"We're on our way up!" Carly replied. She turned to Sam. "You know what to do?"

"Yes," Sam said.

She and Carly both started talking at once,

listing the segments they planned for the Web show.

"You and I stand together, you on the left, me on the right, camera starts on the sign, pans down to us, Freddie points, you say hi to the audience, introduce me, we talk, and then we start showing all the kids with the weird talents," Sam babbled.

Carly wasn't listening. She was running everything over in her mind. "We stand together, me on the left, you on the right, camera opens on the sign, pans down to you and me, Freddie cues us, I welcome the people, then I introduce you, we chat, then we bring out the kids with the crazy talents."

She turned to Sam. "You got it?" Carly asked.

Sam nodded. "I'm down."

The elevator doors opened with a ding. The third floor of Carly and Spencer's loft now held a stage, cool light sculptures, and the front end of a souped-up old car. One of the walls had been painted midnight blue, and the girls had added star lights and a perfect half moon. Spencer had

created an *iCarly* sign and hung it over the big window, right above a neon green sign reading "live."

Freddie had set up his camera equipment and laptop in front of the elevator. He was typing instructions into his computer.

"Twenty seconds," he warned as the girls got off the elevator.

Carly threw him her water bottle and the girls ran to their mark in the center of the room.

Freddie picked up his camera.

"Here we go," Carly said, taking a deep breath to calm herself down.

"I look good?" Sam asked.

"Perfect," Carly answered. "Me?"

Sam checked out her friend. "You've something in your teeth."

"What?" Carly screamed. "Get it out! Get it out!"

Sam used her fingernail to get the gook off Carly's tooth while Freddie counted down. "In six seconds . . . five . . . four . . . three . . . two . . . and . . ." Freddie pointed at Carly, and the girls turned to the camera.

This was it, their first show was about to begin.

"Hey there, people of earth," Carly said with a big smile. "I'm Carly Shay and this is our very first Webcast of a little show we call *iCarly*."

"She's Carly . . ." Sam said, pointing to her friend.

"She's Sam," Carly added.

"Sam I am," Sam said, pointing to herself.

Just to be sure, Carly added one more introduction. "Carly — Sam," she said, pointing first to herself and then at Sam.

"I think they're clear," Sam said.

"Demonstrate the thing!" Carly said.

"Oh yeah!" Sam held up a blue remote control. "With this item, provided by our dorky friend Freddie —"

"That's disrespectful," Freddie yelled from behind the camera.

Sam ignored him. "We can do this," she said, pressing a button on the remote. The room was filled with the sound of cheers and applause. "And this." She pressed another button, and the cheers were replaced with boos. There was one more

button. Sam pressed it and the room was filled with music and glittering lights.

Carly and Sam launched into a dance.

Finally, Sam pressed another button and the music stopped.

"Okay," Carly said, flipping her long, brown hair away from her face. "Tonight we're going to show you some kids with super insane talents."

Sam threw her arms out and danced across the room singing, "*Talent shoooowwww . . .*"

"Stop it," Carly whispered. She turned to the camera.

Carly and Sam had decided earlier to talk to each other the way they always did — cutting in, interrupting, and finishing each other's sentences. That way they wouldn't just look like a couple of boring, talking heads.

"Okay, this first kid we're going to show you can take a glass of milk . . ." Carly said.

". . . this is so deliciously gross . . ." Sam added.

". . . snort the milk up into his nose . . ." Carly continued.

Sam was still raving about how wonderfully gross it was. ". . . it's the best thing ever . . ."

Carly made a face. It was the grossest thing ever, and one of the coolest. ". . . and then make the milk squirt out of his eyes."

"This boy has talent!" Sam said.

"Let's bring him out," Carly said. "Simon Kendal!"

"You're up, dude!" Sam added. She hit the button, and cheers and applause filled the room.

Simon ran out and stood behind a stool with a glass of milk on it. Freddie pulled back and brought all three kids into the camera shot.

"Okay, Simon, you ready to blow people away with your crazy talent?" Carly asked.

"Do it!" Sam urged.

Simon nodded. "Let's go," he said.

Carly turned to Sam. "Drumroll," she said.

Sam hit another button on her remote and a drumroll filled the room.

Freddie focused his lens on Simon. Simon poured some milk into his hand and snorted it up his nose. Then he pulled his lower eyelids down. Freddie zoomed in for a close-up of milk

squirting out of Simon's eyes. A milky tear ran down his cheek.

Freddie zoomed out again to catch Carly's and Sam's reactions for their viewers.

The girls screamed. Sam screamed because she absolutely loved it. Carly screamed because she thought it was the grossest thing ever. They ran over to Simon and stood on either side of him.

"The king of dairy!" Carly said. "The king of dairy!"

"You don't see that every day," Sam added.

Simon bowed with a smile, and then left the stage.

Their next *iCarly* act came out in a pink leotard and did a backbend.

"She's a contortionist!" Carly said, watching the girl stretch one way and then the other before she folded in two. "Would you look at her!"

"I'm looking, and it looks painful!" Sam added.

The girl stood on her head and did a split — upside down!

"That is amazing. She's so stretchy," Sam said.

"Don't you just want to fold her up and put her in your pocket?" Carly asked.

"I'm not normal," the girl joked, before walking offstage on her hands.

"Okay, this is insane!" Sam said about their next act.

A boy stood between her and Carly.

"Tell the people your name," Carly said.

He looked into the camera. "Brennan Yubberly."

"Yubberly!" Carly said.

"Yeah, Yubberly!" Sam added. It was a fun name to say.

Carly introduced his talent. "Okay, any word you say, Brennan can say backwards — perfectly!"

"He's a backwards talker!" Sam added.

"Check this out," Carly said into the camera. "Ointment."

Brennan didn't blink. He didn't even take a second to think about it. "Tnemtnio," he said.

"Yes!" Sam pumped her fist in the air. But that was too easy. She wanted more. "Okay. Slippery watermelon."

"Yreppils nolemretaw," Brennan said.

"Do you hear this?" Carly asked.

"We love this boy!" Sam said.

"Okay, okay," Carly said. Now it was time for a really hard one. "Say, 'I must be from the planet Jupiter because there's no other way I could be saying this backwards!'"

Brennan looked right into the camera. "I tsum eb morf eht tenalp retipuJ esuaceb sereht on rehto yaw I dluoc eb gniyas siht sdrawkcab!"

Carly and Sam screamed in amazement.

"Did you hear that?" Carly asked.

"Insanity!" Sam shouted.

"Ytinasni!" Brennan yelled.

But Sam decided it was time for their next act. "That's enough, Brennan," she said, elbowing him in the side.

The show was a whirlwind of weird and wacky talent. All the acts that Miss Briggs had said no to, the acts that made Carly and Sam crack up in the auditions, had agreed to be on the first episode of *iCarly*.

Sam watched a girl leave the stage with her amazing pet goat — a goat that barked and begged

like a dog. "Whoa, looking at that goat made me hungry."

"Well, you can eat soon because the very first Webcast of *iCarly* is almost over," Carly told her hungry friend.

Sam hit a button on the remote control and a sad "awwwwww" filled the room.

"No, no, don't be sad," Carly said. "We still have one more kid with a strange talent, but first —"

"Here's some stuff you need to know," Sam said.

Carly picked up Sam's thought. "If you liked our show, tell your friends," she said.

"And your cousins, people you like," Sam added.

"People you don't like," Carly joked.

"All the people on this planet," Sam said with a laugh. *Why not dream big*, she thought.

Carly got to the point, which was getting their viewers to tell people about their show, so that they would log on to their computers and watch, too. "Tell everyone that we're going to be here, live, online every week at iCarly-dot-com," Carly said.

"In fact, next week Carly's going to take my tonsils out right here," Sam said.

Carly rolled her eyes. "She's lying."

"But how awesome would that be?" Sam asked.

"So, if there's anything you want to see us do," Carly said.

"Or hear us talk about right here on the show," Sam added.

"No matter how crazy . . ." Carly said.

"Or strange," Sam said.

"You can contact us by going to iCarly-dot-com and clicking on the feedback button."

"Feedback button," Sam sang, dancing across the room.

Carly laughed. "Click till it hurts," she told her audience.

Sam popped her head in front of Carly's. "Oh, and if you want to send us a video," she said.

"Of you doing or saying anything cool," Carly added.

Sam was ready with examples. "Telling a joke, eating a bug."

"Just email the video clip to us," Carly explained.

"Carly and me," Sam said.

"Me and Sam," Carly added.

"At iCarly-dot-com," Sam finished.

"If it's cool enough, we'll show it right here on *iCarly*," Carly said. "So send us stuff!"

"Talk back," Sam urged.

"But be nice, because if you're not," Carly warned.

"We'll find out where you live," Sam teased.

It was time to bring the show to a close with their last act.

"Okay! Our last amazingly talented kid's name is Taryn James, and she's about to play us out."

"With her trumpet," Sam explained.

"But with a little extra twist," Carly laughed. "Hit the button."

Sam filled the room with cheers and applause.

"Get out here, Taryn!" Carly said.

Taryn ran out with her pogo stick and her trumpet. Freddie focused the camera on her as she started to jump. Then she brought the trumpet to her lips and blew. You couldn't call the noise she

i Want More Viewers

created music exactly, but it was still weird and wacky and cool.

"Look at that!" Carly said.

"Who doesn't love that?" Sam asked.

The girls ran to either side of Taryn and jumped up and down, applauding.

"Thanks for watching!" Carly said.

"Tune in next time!" Sam added.

Freddie hit a few buttons on his computer and brought the show to a close. "And we're clear," he announced, lowering the camera.

"We did it!" Sam exclaimed, raising her hand and slapping Carly a high five.

Freddie ran over and they all hugged for a second, until Sam remembered that Freddie was Freddie, and Freddie remembered that Sam was Sam.

But they were all super excited. They had finished their first show, and it was great!

Chapter 7

A couple of hours later, they decided to check and see how many viewers had logged on to catch their show. They had told all their friends to watch, of course, but they also hoped that other kids would find them while they were surfing the Web.

Freddie typed in the address for the Website he had set up at iCarly.com.

"Well?" Carly asked, peering over his shoulder.

"Hurry!" Sam urged.

"You guys are making me nervous!" Freddie said. "Oh, here it is!" he said.

"How many?" Carly asked, peering over his shoulder.

Freddie's jaw dropped. "Thirty-seven thousand!"

All three of them started screaming and jumping up and down. They couldn't believe that thirty-seven thousand people had actually watched their show!

Spencer came in, wearing a T-shirt with a big red S and a tie painted on it. He saw Carly and her friends jumping around and he joined in. "Woo hoo!" he yelled, and then asked, "Why are we happy?"

"Because our very first Web show rocked!" Carly told him.

"And was watched by over thirty-seven thousand people!" Sam said.

"Get out!" Spencer yelled. He pulled Carly toward him and gave her a pat on the head, pretending to be overcome with emotion. "My baby sister's a Web star."

"Hey," Sam said, getting a fabulous idea. "We should have a party. You know, to celebrate."

"Yes. Yes, we should," Spencer agreed. He began to pace. "But it shouldn't be a normal, regular party," he said.

"Oh no," Carly agreed.

"It needs to be something different," Spencer said. "Something," he thought for a moment, "wonderfully random."

Carly had an idea. "Crazy hat party?" she asked.

Spencer snapped his fingers. That was it!

The next night, their loft was full of kids in crazy hats. All of the acts from their first show had shown up. So had a bunch of Carly's friends, and some of Spencer's, too. Everyone wore a wild hat.

Carly had chosen a glittery, blue cowboy hat. She was in the kitchen, searching for a place to set a tray of veggies and dip.

Freddie walked over. The tail of his coonskin cap fell over one shoulder. "Hey, awesome party," he said.

"Yeah," Carly agreed, looking around. Everyone was dancing. They all seemed to be having a good time.

"Hey, cupcake," Sam said. She wore a red, feathery hat with two long antennae.

"There you are," Carly said. "Nice hat!"

"Back at'cha," Sam said with a smile.

Sharon and Krisha, who lived in the building, ran over holding autograph books and pens.

"Hi, um, can we get your autographs?" Sharon asked.

"We love *iCarly*," Krisha added.

Carly and Sam exchanged looks. People wanted their autographs? How weird was that!

"Um, sure," Carly said, taking the pen.

"No prob." Sam scribbled her name on one book and then the other.

"There you go," Carly said, handing Krisha her pen.

"I love you, Carly!" Krisha said, giving Carly a big hug.

Carly and Sam watched the two girls scurry off to look at their autographs.

"Wow," Carly said. She was still a little stunned. "I just signed an autograph."

"Get used to it," Sam warned her. "*iCarly's* a great show. You might get famous."

Carly shook her head. The whole idea struck her as really, really strange. Famous? Her? "Yeah,

I don't know if I'm going to like that," she said, suddenly feeling very shy.

At that moment Tate and Ricky, two totally cute guys from school, walked over.

"Hey. Saw your Web show," Tate said. "Pretty cool."

Carly and Sam exchanged grins. Tate had actually watched their show!

"Thanks," Carly said.

"Yeah, thanks a lot," Sam agreed.

"So, you guys want to dance?" Tate asked.

"Yes!" Carly said.

"Cool, let's do it!" Sam answered at the same time.

The four of them joined the rest of the party on the dance floor.

Carly turned to her friend. Maybe fame wasn't going to be strange. Maybe it was going to be great. "I'm going to like it," Carly told Sam with a smile. Then she took her hat off and threw it up into the air!

I'm going to like it a lot, she thought.

part TWO

iWant More
Viewers

Chapter 1

For Carly, Sam, and Freddie, the weekly *iCarly* live Webcast was beginning to feel like a regular part of their lives. They were in the middle of their third show, and it was awesome. Carly and Sam stood in the center of the studio and faced Freddie and his handheld camera.

"Okay! Next on *iCarly*, we're going to talk about the doorman who works in the lobby of this building," Carly said. Her face automatically screwed up as if she had smelled something horrible — that's what usually happened when she thought about the doorman. "His name is Lewbert."

Sam jumped in front of the camera. "The meanest man alive," she added.

"We asked our technical producer Freddie —"

Sam interrupted. "Say yo to the people, Freddie."

Freddie turned his camera around and pointed it at himself. "Yo to the people!" he said. "How y'all doing out there —"

Sam cut him off by turning his camera back on herself. "That's enough, Freddie," she said.

Freddie rolled his eyes.

"Anyway, we've been secretly videotaping Lewbert for almost a week," Carly explained.

"So, let's take a look at some of the highlights," Sam said.

"Freddie, roll the clip," Carly finished.

Sam pushed a button on her remote control. A flat screen TV attached to a robotic arm popped out from the wall.

Freddie put his camera down and ran his fingers over the track pad of his computer. "Playback," he said, pushing some buttons.

A picture of Lewbert in his doorman's uniform appeared on the screen. He was slumped at his desk, reading a magazine.

"Okay, and there's Lewbert sitting at his desk," Carly said.

Sam didn't like Lewbert. She had had way too many run-ins with the doorman when she came to visit her friend. "Just a rude little man working in the lobby," she said.

"If you look real close, you can see his wart. Zoom in on it, Freddie," Carly said.

Freddie clicked some buttons on his laptop. "Digital zoom," he announced.

The camera zoomed in on the doorman. What looked like a small brown smudge before was now plainly visible. Lewbert had a humungous grayish-brown wart on his cheek.

"There it is," Carly said. "Living happily right on Lewbert's face."

"I call that wart Little Lewbert," Sam joked.

They all watched as Lewbert stuck his finger in his ear and started digging around for earwax.

Carly shuddered. Lewbert in person was bad enough, but somehow looking at him, his wart, and his earwax up close was positively disgusting. "Zoom out, Freddie," she said.

Freddie worked his controls, zooming back out to a normal view of the lobby.

Carly thought their next Lewbert highlight was even funnier. Their secret camera showed a woman walking across the lobby holding a little,

white, fluffy dog. "Okay, see that lady there? Watch what happens," Carly said.

The woman walked to the mailboxes in the lobby and slipped a key into one of the boxes.

Lewbert came up behind her. "Out!" he screamed.

The dog started barking at him.

"I just need to get my mail," the woman explained.

"No dogs in my lobby!" he insisted.

"I'll leave in a minute!" the woman said indignantly.

"Now! Out!" Lewbert screamed.

The dog started barking at the doorman, and the doorman barked back.

The woman had to shout to be heard above her dog and the doorman. "You know what? I pay rent in this building. This isn't right!" she insisted.

Lewbert didn't care. He kept barking at the dog and he chased the woman out of the lobby — without her mail.

The woman yelled as she ran. "I can't believe you're treating us like this."

Sam shook her head in amazement. "He's arguing with a Pomegranate," she said.

"Pomeranian," Carly corrected.

Sam shrugged. "Whatever. It's a dog!"

The next Lewbert clip was even funnier, and a perfect example of just how mean Lewbert could be.

"Okay, now watch Lewbert closely," Carly said.

A man and a woman were talking in the middle of the lobby. A sweet little boy stood next to them, holding a balloon and eating a cookie.

"See that little kid with a balloon?" Sam asked.

They watched on the monitor as Lewbert snuck up behind the boy and grabbed his cookie. Then the doorman shoved it whole into his mouth before the boy could do or say anything to stop him.

"Mommy! That man ate my cookie!" the little boy cried.

The woman turned on the doorman. "You took my son's cookie?" she asked.

Lewbert's mouth was full of cookie. "No!" he said, spewing cookie crumbs on her as he

73

talked. "How dare you! Don't you accuse me of stealing no cookie," he insisted. The cookie crumbs gave him away. With every syllable, crumbs shot out of his mouth. They landed all over him and hit the poor woman in the face.

Carly grinned. Only Lewbert was mean enough to steal a little kid's cookie and then lie about it with cookie crumbs spewing all over the place.

"You are so mean!" the woman said. "You have crumbs falling over your face and now they're all over my face." She held up a hand to shield herself.

Lewbert imitated the woman, making fun of her. The man she had been talking to called for building security.

A security guard ran down the steps.

"Security, that man took my son's cookie, what are you going to do about it?" the woman demanded.

Stealing the little boy's cookie wasn't enough for Lewbert. While the man and woman were

telling the security guard their side of the story, the doorman reached behind his desk and grabbed an umbrella. He used the pointy tip to poke a hole in the boy's balloon.

Freddie ended the clip with the image of the boy screaming about his popped balloon, and then he turned the camera on the girls.

"Did you see that?" Carly said into the camera.

"You see what he did?" Sam asked.

"As you can see," Carly explained, "Lewbert is a bad person."

"Not a good dude," Sam agreed. "Which is why we're introducing a new segment on *iCarly* which we call . . ."

The girls looked into the camera and announced in unison. "'Messin' with Lewbert'!"

Freddie clicked a button on his computer and a graphic that read "Messin' with Lewbert" over a freeze frame of Lewbert's face.

"Okay, there's Lewbert live," Carly said, as Freddie switched to the Live Lewbert Cam hidden in the lobby.

Lewbert sat behind his desk, reading a magazine.

Sam picked up the phone. "I'll dial the lobby downstairs," she said.

Lewbert's phone rang and he picked it up.

"Main lobby," he said into the phone.

Sam held the telephone receiver so that it was facing Carly. Carly pulled an air horn from behind her back, held it up to the phone, and let it rip.

They watched Lewbert jump back with a scream. The phone went flying, and Lewbert landed on the floor.

Normally, Carly would think that prank was too mean. But they had just watched the doorman steal a little boy's cookie and then pop his balloon. If anyone deserved an air horn in his ear, it was Lewbert.

"And that concludes this segment of 'Messin' with Lewbert,'" Carly said with a laugh.

Sam was laughing, too.

They turned back to the Live Lewbert Cam to watch the doorman pull himself up off the floor and grab the phone again. "Who is this?" he asked, plainly furious.

Sam casually held the phone up again and Carly raised the air horn.

Hooooooooonnnnnk!

Lewbert stumbled back against the wall and hit the floor with a loud, satisfying *thwack*!

Chapter 2

After the show, Carly made spaghetti and meatballs for dinner. Sam was helping, sort of, while Freddie updated the *iCarly* Website.

He ran into the kitchen and jumped onto a stool. "What-up, m'peeps?"

"Wow, that greeting was uncool in so many ways," Sam said with a deadpan expression.

Freddie never could ignore Sam's insults. "Yeah? Well, 'uncool' is the new cool," he told her.

"Wow, that comeback was uncool in so many ways," Sam said with the same deadpan expression.

Freddie started to get mad. "All right, you know what, Sam?" he yelled.

This is too easy, Sam thought. "What, Freddie?" Sam teased. "Why don't you tell me what?"

"I am a human being, and I deserve respect," Freddie yelled.

"Oh, you're a human being?" Sam asked. "You deserve a new brain."

Carly rolled her eyes. There they went — again! Sam insulted Freddie. Freddie got mad. Sam insulted Freddie some more. Freddie got madder. Carly was the one who always got stuck playing peacemaker between them.

"At least *I have* a brain!" Freddie responded.

"Oh no, you don't have a brain, you have nose hairs —"

Carly had come up with a new plan to get them to stop. She picked up a spray bottle, walked over to her friends, and spritzed water directly into their faces.

Freddie and Sam stopped arguing and stared at Carly as if she were crazy.

"What'd you just do?" Sam asked.

Freddie covered his face. "What was that?"

"Oh, see, when you have a cat, that's how you get them to stop misbehaving," Carly explained. "You just spritz them with some water."

Cat? Sam and Freddie exchanged confused looks.

"Well, you can't do that to us," Sam said.

"We're not cats," Freddie told her.

For once Sam agreed with Freddie on something. "Yeah," she said. "Just put your little bottle —"

Carly spritzed them both again and they stopped objecting. They also stopped yelling at each other.

Now that that was settled, Carly called for her brother. "Spencer! Dinnertime!" Then she turned to her now-quiet friends. "You guys staying?" she asked.

Sam shrugged. "Yeah, I got no place to go."

"Sure, thanks," Freddie said.

They set the table together. Sam grabbed the plates to set the table. Freddie reached for the glasses.

Spencer ran in, carrying a toilet seat. "I'm here," he said, and then he realized that a toilet seat might not be welcome at the dinner table. "One sec," he said, running into the back room again.

Carly and her friends watched him go. They had learned to stop asking questions about Spencer's bizarro props. You never knew what he was going to turn into a sculpture. Carly just hoped he wouldn't turn that toilet seat into a frame for her picture.

"So what's for dinner?" Spencer asked, coming back empty-handed.

"We're having my special spaghetti," Carly announced.

Sam and Spencer had both had Carly's spaghetti before, and they didn't think it was so special.

Freddie was more enthusiastic. "Nice-looking meatballs!" he said, spearing one with his fork before passing the bowl to Spencer.

Spencer started filling his plate. "Hey, you guys' Web show was pretty awesome tonight." He chuckled, thinking about the Lewbert segment. "I loved how you guys zoomed in on Lewbert's big old wart. I wonder what would happen if you squeezed that thing. You think some kind of Lewberty goo would squirt out of it?"

81

Freddie was about to pop a meatball in his mouth. But somehow the words "Lewberty goo" came with a visual picture. Gross! He dropped the meatball and swallowed.

"I just wish we could get more people watching the show," Sam said.

"The same number of people watched *iCarly* this week as last week," Freddie told them. There was frustration in his voice. He thought word would spread and the number of viewers who logged in each week would jump. But that hadn't happened.

"That's the problem," Sam said. "Our show's getting better and better, so more people should be watching it."

Spencer thought they were making the show every week because it was fun, not because they wanted a lot of people to watch. "Why do you guys care how many people are watching?" he asked.

Freddie was shocked that Spencer had even asked that question. "Why do we care?" he asked. Of course they wanted lots of people to watch. Why make a show if no one watched?

Sam had the perfect comparison to explain the situation to Spencer. "You're an artist. When you create a new sculpture, do you want two people to see it, or do you want two million people to see it?"

"Two million," Spencer admitted, a little embarrassed.

"So . . . ideas?" Carly asked.

"Yeah," Sam said. "Your spaghetti could use more garlic."

"I think Carly's spaghetti is great," Freddie said, defending his crush and her cooking.

"Then why don't you put some under your pillow," Sam said with a snide expression.

"Because maybe I don't want to put pasta under my pillow!" Freddie yelled. "Maybe you should try —"

Sam cut him off. "Does that sound like a good idea to you? I think it sounds like a good idea —"

Carly cut them both off with her spray bottle, spritzing them both in the face. "All right, look," she said, when they had stopped yelling at each other. "We know that making a good show is important."

"And so is getting more people to watch," Sam added.

"Okay, so what if we each think of a cool way to get more people to watch," Carly suggested.

"Yeah?" Sam said, waiting for the rest.

"And then we show our ideas to the *iCarly* audience," Carly said.

Freddie knew where she was going with this. They were all about making the show interactive, so that their viewers would feel like they were part of it all. "And we have them vote on who came up with the best idea?" he asked.

"Right," Carly agreed. "Like a contest. That way we do a good show *and* get more viewers."

"I'm on Carly's team," Sam said immediately.

"Whoa, teams? She said *each*," Freddie pointed out. "And why do you get to be on Carly's team?"

"Because *each* sounds like a lot of work," Sam answered.

"Relax, buddy," Spencer said to Freddie. "I'll be on your team."

"Seriously?" Carly asked. Spencer was usually so busy, she didn't think he'd be up for an *iCarly*

84

contest. But it would definitely be more fun if he was a part of it.

"Yeah, I got time," Spencer said.

Sam was surprised, too. Spencer had been busy lately, with a new friend. "You're not still dating that girl?" she asked.

"Nah, she only liked me for my socks," Spencer admitted.

Sam was confused. Did Spencer really say that a girl had liked him for his socks? "That's weird," she said.

"Is it?" Spencer asked knowingly. He put his foot on the table and pulled up his pants leg. He was wearing orange-and-yellow-striped socks. They had neon blue and purple squiggling lines running up and down the sides.

Freddie took one look at Spencer's socks and realized he might have gotten a better deal than Sam. "Well okay then, we're partners," he said to Spencer.

"Partners!" Spencer agreed, giving Freddie a fist bump.

"Perfect," Carly said. "So it's me and Sam

versus Freddie and Spencer. The team with the best idea to get more viewers wins."

"Okay," Freddie agreed. "But I think the team that loses should have some penalty."

"Hasn't life already penalized you enough?" Sam asked innocently.

Carly picked up the water bottle and spritzed Sam in the face before another fight could break out. "That's for being mean," she said.

Sam wiped her face with a napkin. The thing was, she enjoyed being mean to Freddie. And he made it so easy. "It was worth it," she admitted.

"All right, c'mon," Spencer said. "What should the losers have to do?"

Carly thought about it for a minute. "I'm going to say the losing team has to . . ." She broke into a huge smile as the perfect idea came to her. ". . . touch Lewbert's wart!"

"Yeah!" Spencer yelled. Then he looked around and saw the complete disgust on the other three faces at the table. "I mean uggghhh," he said quietly.

86

Chapter 3

Freddie was getting a book out of his locker at school the next day when Spencer came racing in. Carly's brother had gotten an excellent idea for the contest, and there was no way he could wait until school let out to share it with Freddie.

Spencer ran down the hall, then spotted his partner. "Hey, Freddie," he yelled.

Startled, Freddie straightened up and slammed his head on the top of his locker. "Ow! Man!" he cried, grabbing his head.

"What'cha doing?" Spencer asked.

"Bleeding," Freddie answered with a sarcastic expression. "Why are you here?"

"We are going to win the contest," Spencer told him. "I came up with an insanely awesome way to get more people watching your Webcast."

Spencer's excitement was contagious. Freddie forgot all about the new lump on his head. "Tell me!"

"We get a bunch of fireworks, right?" Spencer said.

Freddie nodded.

"And not the lightweight consumer-grade stuff. I'm talking Fourth of July razzle-dazzle," Spencer said.

Freddie's eyes lit up. "Razzle-dazzle?"

"Yes, both," Spencer told him. "Then, at night, we launch the fireworks off the roof of our building, and they explode spelling out 'iCarly-dot-com' in the sky."

Freddie watched Spencer practically draw a picture with his words. He saw a huge *iCarly* sign in the sky. "Can we really do that?" he asked.

"No," Spencer admitted. His first idea was all about the razzle-dazzle, but when he realized that that feat was impossible, he looked for another idea. And he found one. "I came up with something else: a sign."

Freddie slumped against the lockers. "A sign?"

he asked. Anyone could make a sign. That wasn't going to win any contest.

"A big sign," Spencer told him. "One that lights up all different colors and says, 'Please go online to iCarly-dot-com.'"

Freddie thought about it for a minute. "Yeah yeah, that's good," he agreed. "We should hang it someplace like, uh . . ." He thought about a place where lots and lots of people would see it. "Like over a really busy highway!" he said, snapping his fingers. "Thousands of people will see it when they drive by."

"You are a tiny genius," Spencer said, raising his hand for a high five.

At that moment, Miss Briggs came out of her classroom. She stopped and sniffed when she saw Spencer. "Well, well," she sneered. "Look what the janitor swept up. Spencer Shay."

Spencer merely smiled. Miss Briggs couldn't hurt him anymore.

"I thought I'd seen the last of you eight years ago when you graduated," Miss Briggs told him. "But sadly, you're back."

"Nice to see you, Miss Briggs," Spencer said sweetly. "Or, now that I'm older, may I call you Margaret?"

"No, you may not!" Miss Briggs said sharply.

"Why?" Spencer asked innocently.

"My name is Francine!" she yelled.

Spencer and Freddie shared an "uh-oh" look.

Miss Briggs pointed to the doors. "Now get out of here before I give you detention," she yelled.

Spencer shook his head calmly. "I'm twenty-six. You can't give me detention."

Freddie grinned. It was fun to watch someone stand up to Miss Briggs. Someone she couldn't punish anyway. Spencer was right; Miss Briggs couldn't give him detention.

But Miss Briggs had other weapons at her disposal, and she didn't mind using them. She turned to Freddie. "Then I give you detention. One week," she announced.

Freddie gasped. That wasn't fair! "What?" he asked.

Spencer scoffed at the teacher. "You don't scare him," he said, pointing to Freddie.

Freddie nudged Spencer. "Yeah she does," Freddie told him.

Miss Briggs smiled, happy to be scaring someone. She glared at Spencer. "Get out!" she demanded.

Spencer glared back. He had a right to be there. He was conferring with his partner about a very important contest. "No," he said.

Miss Briggs turned on Freddie again. "Two weeks detention," she spat.

"Dude! Get out of here!" Freddie pleaded. He grabbed Spencer by the shirt and started pulling him to the doors.

"N-n-n-n-n-no, wait," Spencer insisted. "I am not letting this lady push me —"

Miss Briggs cut him off. "Spencer Shay, you have thirty seconds to leave or else Freddie gets expelled," she said, checking her watch.

Expelled?

"Goooooo!" Freddie screamed, pushing Spencer all the way out of the door.

☺ ☺ ☺ ☺ ☺

Carly was doing her homework in the living room when Sam rushed in.

"I got it! I got it!" Sam yelled.

Carly dropped her notebook and jumped to her feet. "You thought of an idea for the contest?" she asked, relieved and excited. So far she hadn't come up with anything that would definitely win the contest. Seeing Lewbert's warty face when she came home from school had filled her with dread. What if Spencer and Freddie came up with a better idea? She'd have to touch that horrible thing. What if it was contagious?

"No, you remember at lunch, that piece of corn I got stuck in my teeth?" Sam asked.

Carly looked at her friend as if she were crazy. Was Sam seriously asking her about corn? "No," Carly admitted.

Sam held up her finger. A tiny piece of corn sat on its tip. "Well here it is!" she announced, and then flicked the corn onto the floor.

"And thank you for flicking your used corn onto my floor," Carly said.

Sam flopped onto the couch and picked up a magazine.

"Now give me that," Carly said, taking it away from her again. "You've got to help me think of an idea."

"All right," Sam said, rolling her eyes. As far as she was concerned, Carly was way too stressed about this contest. Sam did some deep thinking for one second, came up with nothing, and picked up the remote control. "Right after we watch *Seattle Beat*," she said.

"No," Carly said.

"Please?" Sam whined.

"Give me the remote!" Carly said, pulling it out of Sam's hands and holding it out of arm's reach.

Sam leaned over her and tried to yank it back. "Give it to me!" Sam said.

Carly wouldn't let go. "Give it! Let go!"

"Give it to me!" Sam insisted. "You're hurting my finger."

Carly wasn't sympathetic. "Well, then, move your finger," she told Sam. "Let go of the remote, Sam!"

But Sam wouldn't let go. "You let go! You let go!" she insisted. "*Pleeeease!*" she whined again. "*Pleeeease!*"

93

Carly threw her arms up in frustration. "Okay, fine!" she yelled.

Sam turned on the television and switched channels until she found *Seattle Beat*. *Seattle Beat* was one of their favorite television shows. All the cool local Seattle bands, like Carly's favorite, Cuddle Fish, appeared on the show. Carly and Sam had even joined the group of teens that hung outside the show's big windows a couple of times so that they could see their favorite acts up close and personal.

The hostess, Bianca Jay, was pretty cool, too. ". . . okay, you may like the old drummer better," Bianca was saying into the camera. "But I still say they're one of the best bands happening in Seattle today."

The teens around her and the crowd outside the window hooted and hollered in agreement.

"And to prove it," Bianca continued, "you're going to see them right here on *Seattle Beat* live — coming up in less than a half hour." She eyed the group around her. "Is that cool?" she asked.

The kids in the studio cheered.

Sam and Carly shouted "Woo hoo!" along with them, a little sarcastically. They were convinced that if they were ever on *Seattle Beat*, there's no way they would act as dorky as the kids in the studio.

"And how about you people outside the *Seattle Beat* window?" Bianca asked.

The crowd outside the window cheered wildly. A few of them held up signs and jumped up and down. One sign said "Seattle Beat," another read "I ♥ Cuddle Fish."

Carly's eyes widened. That was it! She had an amazing idea. She grabbed the remote from Sam and pushed the mute button. "I got it. I know how we're going to get a ton more people to watch the Webcast."

"Does it involve dental floss?" Sam asked.

Once again, Carly had to look at her friend and wonder if she was totally insane. "No, why?"

"I think that piece of corn had a friend," she said, picking at her teeth.

Carly grabbed Sam's wrists to get her to focus. "Listen! You see those people outside the window on *Seattle Beat*?" she said.

95

"Yeah?" Sam asked, wondering where this was going and hoping it didn't include work.

"You and I are going to make a big banner," Carly said excitedly.

Sam nodded, warming up to the idea. "I enjoy big banners," she admitted.

"And we're going to take it to *Seattle Beat* and hold it up right in front of that window for this whole city to see," Carly told her.

"That's brilliant," Sam told her. "Everybody watches *Seattle Beat*."

Carly grinned. "Uh-huh." She wasn't going to have to touch Lewbert's wart after all! Spencer and Freddie would definitely lose the bet.

"Well, say thank you," Sam prompted her.

"Why?" Carly asked. "I thought of it."

"Yeah, but I thought of watching TV," Sam explained.

Carly rolled her eyes. "Let's just go make the banner." She turned off the TV and headed for the stairs.

"All right," Sam agreed, starting to follow her. "Let's banner it up." She watched Carly run up the

stairs and then flopped back onto the couch, reaching for the TV remote again.

Carly came back with her water bottle and sprayed Sam in the back of her head.

"Okay, okay," Sam said, holding up her hand to block the water spritzes.

Carly kept spraying until Sam was on her feet and running up the stairs.

"I'm coming, okay!" Sam said.

Carly ran behind her. It was always better to stay behind Sam and be ready to give her a prod when work was involved.

Chapter 4

After school the next day, Carly and Sam ran to the TV studio with a big, colorful sign that read:

"Hurry!" Carly urged. "It's about to rain."

"I'm right behind you," Sam said, looking up at the gray sky. She heard thunder, and then felt a drop. "And it's already raining."

Big drops were falling when they reached the

Seattle Beat windows. There was already a crowd in front of the windows when the girls arrived.

Carly worked her way forward as politely as possible. "Excuse us," she said. "Can we please get through there?" No one moved. Carly had to start jostling her way through the people. "Pardon," she said, stepping on someone's foot. "Excuse me. Coming through."

Sam didn't share Carly's need to be polite. "Move!" she ordered. "Out of my way. Banner on the move." She glared at someone blocking her path. "Don't touch me. Step aside!"

Finally, they made their way to the front of the crowd. They could see Bianca Jay, hosting the live show. Thunder roared overhead and it started to rain harder.

"Hold it up high!" Carly told Sam. She wanted to be sure the sign would be readable behind the host of the show.

"Let's spread the word, baby," Sam agreed, holding the sign up. She turned to a boy blocking their banner. "Move!" she yelled. "We're from the Internet!"

The boy took one look at Sam and scurried off.

Carly laughed. "Get ready, Seattle!" she yelled.

She and Sam held the sign directly in front of the window. Anyone watching *Seattle Beat* would see their sign. They didn't even mind the rain and wind, and stayed in place even when half the crowd ran for cover.

Lightning and thunder crashed overhead while Carly and Sam tried to hold up their banner for everyone to see. The girls were drenched, but it was worth it if it meant they would win the contest. They danced to the music coming from inside the studio and pointed to their sign.

The music video being played on the air came to an end.

Bianca Jay looked into the camera. "If you like what you just heard, you can catch that band live at The Showbox next weekend."

Bianca Jay looked out the window and saw Carly and Sam's big banner. Only you couldn't read it anymore. The downpour made the letters run. All the paint and Magic Marker had run together, and it was now just a big swirl of muddy colors.

"That sign is messed up!" Bianca Jay said into the camera.

Carly and Sam looked down at their banner, and saw the mess it had become. It wasn't readable at all. "Awwwwwwww," they moaned together.

Carly looked at Sam. Their destroyed sign meant just one thing. "We're going to have to touch Lewbert's wart," she said sadly.

Meanwhile, Spencer and Freddie were at the loft, completely dry, putting the finishing touches on their giant light-up sign.

"Okay, I've got the ground wire attached," Freddie said, picking up a wrench. "Let's see if we've got a hot circuit."

"No-no-no-no-no-no-no," Spencer yelled, jumping up from behind the sign.

"Why no?" Freddie asked. "Seven times?"

"Because you're a child, and this is high volt-age stuff." Spencer took the wrench from Freddie and pointed to his plastic goggles. "And you're not even wearing safety goggles." He reached for the

wires on the back of the sign. "See, you've got to be extra careful when —"

Bzzzztttt!

Spencer had grabbed the wrong wires. Freddie could only watch while Spencer vibrated with electricity for a few seconds until he managed to pull away.

"And that is why we wear safety goggles," Spencer mumbled.

Carly and Sam came in then, completely wet and totally bedraggled. They had passed Lewbert on their way in. He yelled at them for dripping on his floor, and all Carly could think about was the fact that she was going to have to touch that enormous, disgusting wart. What if Spencer was right? What if disgusting Lewberty goo squirted out?

Carly said hello to her brother and Freddie and then sniffed the air. "Do I smell barbecue?" she asked.

"No," Spencer admitted, "that's my burning flesh."

"What's that?" Freddie asked, pointing at the wet paper in the girls' hands.

"Soggy banner." Carly sighed. "Our plan to get more viewers didn't go so well," she admitted.

That was an understatement, Sam thought. It was a complete disaster. "Yeah, like how the *Titanic* staying afloat didn't go so well," she said.

"Oh c'mon, maybe a few people read our sign," Carly said. "Before the rain ruined our hard work and made us sad," she added.

"Yeah," Sam agreed. She didn't want Freddie to be too confident. "We could still win," she told him.

But Freddie was convinced he and Spencer would win the bet. "Yeah, I don't think so," he told Sam. "I think me and Spencer are going to win, and you two are going to have to touch Lewbert's wart."

As much as Freddie wanted to beat Sam, he didn't want Carly to be defeated. "I feel bad for you, Carly," he told her. Then he turned to Sam and narrowed his eyes. "Not for you."

Sam grabbed her sopping wet hair, pushed it into Freddie's face, and gave it a squeeze.

"Sore loser," Freddie said, pushing her away and grabbing a towel to dry his face.

103

"You haven't won yet," Sam pointed out.

"Yeah, what are you guys planning to do?" Carly asked.

"Oh, you'll find out," Spencer said coyly.

"Now, if you'll excuse us, we have a contest to win," Freddie said. "No offense, Carly."

Carly's shoulders slumped. An image of Lewbert's wart popped into her mind again and she shook herself to make it go away. "C'mon, let's go dry off," Carly said to Sam.

The two of them trudged toward the stairs.

"Remember, *iCarly* goes live in three hours," she reminded Freddie and Spencer.

"We'll be ready," Spencer told her.

"To win," Freddie added confidently. "Still no offense, Carly."

As soon as the girls had left the room, Spencer was ready to move the sign. "All right, kid, help me get this puppy down to the lobby," he said.

"Okay, but then I've got to come back up here and get ready for the show," Freddie said.

Spencer took one end of the sign, and Freddie the other. They were moving it toward the door

when Spencer's cell phone rang. They set down the sign again.

"Who's that?" Freddie asked.

Spencer checked his screen. "It's my buddy with the truck," he said. "Hey, are you downstairs?" he said into the phone.

Freddie moved behind the sign and tried to hold it up, but it was too heavy for him. It fell over, trapping him between the couch and the sign.

"Okay, we'll bring it downstairs, then me and you can load it on the back of your truck," Spencer said into his phone. "Okay, down in five." He hung up and said, "Now let's get this sign on the road."

He looked around, searching for his partner. "Freddie? Yo, Fred-o?" Spencer called.

Freddie was wedged under the sign, unable to move. He finally wrestled one of his arms free. It popped above the sign. Freddie waved, trying to get Spencer's attention. "Help . . . me," he called in a weak voice.

Finally Spencer spotted him. He lifted the sign off and together they carried it downstairs to the waiting truck.

105

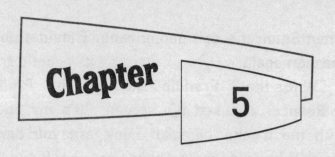
A couple of hours later, Carly and Sam were still wondering what Spencer and Freddie had planned. They were in the middle of their Webcast, and Freddie hadn't spilled the beans. He had the camera trained on Carly.

"Okay, on our last Webcast, Sam and I told you to go to iCarly-dot-com and click that feedback button," she said into the camera.

Sam popped her head into the shot, next to Carly, as planned. "And man, you people clicked on that thing like it was your job!"

"So first, we want to say thanks," Carly said.

She and Sam put their heads together and sang, "Thaaaaaaaanks!"

"And second," Carly added. "We want to show you a video clip sent in by three *iCarly* viewers from Denver, Colorado."

"Freddie, play that clip," Sam said. She pushed

a button on the remote control she held and the flat screen TV moved forward on its robotic arm.

"Some people might say please," Freddie told her.

Sam shrugged. "Yeah, I didn't," she told him.

"Playback," Freddie said, putting down the camera and bringing the clip up on his laptop. Then he cued it to play on the TV screen so that Carly and Sam could watch it along with their viewers.

Three boys appeared on the screen. Two of them were dressed normally, but the one in the middle was wearing a fuzzy pink bunny suit, complete with enormous, pink and white bunny ears. Only his face was visible.

"Hey, Carly and Sam," said the guy in the bunny suit. "We love your Web show."

The other two guys pointed at the camera. "Love it! Yeah!" they said. "Woo hoo! Carly and Sam!"

"Okay, okay," said the guy in the bunny suit, calming his friends down. "We've got an important question. Can you DRINK spaghetti and meatballs?" he asked.

"Spaghetti and meatballs!" his friends shouted. "Spaghetti and meatballs!"

Sam clicked her remote and the screen went dark. The girls turned back to Freddie's hand-held camera.

"Okay, we have no idea why that guy in the middle was wearing a bunny suit," Carly admitted.

"But it did get our attention," Sam said.

"And so did the question: Can you DRINK spaghetti and meatballs?" Carly said.

Sam put her face right up to the camera and said, "We're gonna find out!"

Freddie trailed the girls with his camera as they walked across the studio. A big plate of spaghetti and meatballs sat on a table next to a blender.

"Okay," Carly explained. "We invited the boy who lives two floors down to come up and be our little tester."

"So get out here, Emmett!" Sam said. She pushed a button on her remote and filled the studio with applause and cheers.

Seven-year-old Emmett came out and faced the camera.

"This is Emmett. He doesn't talk much," Carly said.

"Isn't that right?" Sam asked him.

Emmett only nodded.

"See?" Sam said into the camera.

"But luckily, Emmett will eat or drink anything," Carly said. "Seriously, one time Sam dropped a quarter and Emmett ate it."

"I got it back three days later," Sam said, making a face.

Emmett smiled. He was kind of proud of that.

"Okay, Emmett," Carly said. "We want to know. Can you drink spaghetti and meatballs?"

Emmett shrugged and held out his hands as if to say, *How would I know?*

Sam picked up the bowl of spaghetti. "So first, we're going to take this spaghetti."

"And the meatballs," Carly added, picking one up. "You've got to love spherical meat."

"We put it in the blender," Sam said, spooning the spaghetti into the container.

"And there we go," Carly said, dropping in a meatball.

"Ready?" Sam asked, snapping on the blender's lid.

Carly nodded. "And press *frappé*," she said, hitting the button.

The whir of the blender filled the studio for a moment, and then Carly carefully poured the newly blended concoction into a plastic cup.

"Are you ready, kid?" Sam asked Emmett.

Emmett nodded.

Carly handed him the cup. "Go for it," she said.

Emmett took a swig, swallowed, and then faced the camera with a big smile.

Sam pressed the applause button on her remote. "And there you have it," she said into the camera.

"You *can* drink spaghetti and meatballs," Carly said.

"Now get out of here, Emmett," Sam said. "You weird me out."

Emmett smiled again, clearly happy at that news. Before he left he pointed to the cup and looked up at Carly.

"Yes, you can have the rest," Carly told him.

Emmett grinned again. He grabbed the blender, too, and walked out with his liquid spaghetti and meatballs. Carly was just relieved that she wouldn't have to taste it herself.

They showed more funny video clips sent in by their viewers and then it was time to clue them in to what Carly, Sam, and Freddie had been up to in the last week.

"Okay, now we're going to do something we've never done before," Carly said.

"Tell us what it is, Carly!" Sam said, pretending to be enthusiastic. She was sort of dreading the fact that Freddie was going to win.

Freddie zoomed in and moved the camera from one girl to the other, as they explained what was coming next.

"We thought it would be fun to have a contest," Carly said.

Sam nodded. "Carly and me against our technical producer, Freddie."

"Who teamed up with my older brother Spencer," Carly explained.

"To see which team could come up with the best idea to get more people to watch *iCarly*," Sam said.

Freddie zoomed back, and both Carly and Sam were in the shot together.

"Sadly, our plan didn't go too great," Carly told them.

"Check it out," Sam said, hitting the button on her remote that brought the TV screen forward again.

Freddie brought up the clip of the girls at *Seattle Beat*. Carly and Sam watched themselves in the window, waving and smiling as they got wetter and wetter, completely oblivious to the fact that their sign was turning into a rainbow of colors — unreadable colors.

They relived the moment when Bianca Jay looked out the window and made fun of the big banner they had worked so hard on.

"That sign is messed up," Bianca Jay had said into the *Seattle Beat* camera.

Freddie stopped the clip and swung the camera back to Carly and Sam.

"Okay, obviously, that sign won't be getting us any new viewers," Carly said.

"Our project failed." Sam pressed the "awwwwwww" button on her remote. "But luckily, we weren't the only ones with a plan this week."

"So let's go to my brother, Spencer, live on a remote camera to tell us about his and Freddie's idea," Carly announced.

"Okay, going to Spencer live," Freddie said, typing onto his laptop.

An image on the television flickered, and then Spencer appeared. He was next to a busy highway, staring into space, and eating a taco.

"Hey, Spencer, how's it going out there?" Carly asked.

"What's up, Spence?" Sam said.

Spencer took another big bite of his taco and watched the cars zoom past.

"Spencer?" Carly said again. "Put the taco down!"

Sam tried hard to get his attention, too. "Uh, helllooo? Are you there?"

Carly turned to Freddie. "Can he hear us?" she asked.

"Yeah, he should be able to." Freddie looked at his laptop. "Oh," he said, keying in instructions. "Try now."

Carly yelled this time. "Hey, Spencer!"

Startled, Spencer jumped and dropped his taco. He looked into the remote camera that he had mounted on the overpass earlier. "Oh, hey, Carly! Sam! You guys owe me half a taco."

"Yeah," Carly said quickly. Had Spencer forgotten this was a *live* Webcast? She didn't want to talk about tacos. "So tell us what you're planning to do out there."

"Well, I'm currently standing here by the interstate near the Lumford on-ramp in downtown Seattle," Spencer explained. "Now, as you can see, there are literally many cars. Oh, I'll show you," he added, tilting the remote camera so that it focused on the traffic below him. Cars were zooming in both directions.

"There are literally many passing by every minute, which makes this the perfect place to hang a gigantic, luminescent sign," Spencer said. "Like this!" Spencer pressed a button on an elaborate remote control and moved out of the way.

The giant sign blinked and came to life. Its very bright message read:

PLEASE GO ONLINE TO iCARLY.COM

"Behold the sign!" Spencer said, popping back in front of the camera. "Are you beholding it?"

"Oh, we're beholding it," Carly answered. She was more than a little stunned by the sheer size of the sign, not to mention how bright and colorful it was.

"And since we're good sports, I have to say that sign does deserve a —" Sam pressed her remote control so that Spencer and their audience would hear cheers and applause.

"Good job, Spencer," Carly said. "You too, Freddie."

"Thank you, Carly," Freddie said graciously. "In your face, Sam."

Sam sneered back at him.

Spencer popped back on the monitor. "Carly, Sam, you cannot understand how awesome this sign looks from out here," he raved. "It is so dazzlingly bright, I swear it's like —"

Suddenly they heard the sounds of tires screeching, followed by a loud crunch.

Spencer's expression changed from proud to scared.

"What's going on out there, Spencer?" Carly asked, concerned.

"Well, it seems the sign is so bright and dazzling, it distracted one of the drivers below," Spencer admitted.

There were more screeching tires, followed by thuds and the sound of metal crunching. Horns began to honk.

Spencer tried to explain. "Actually, two of the drivers below —" There was the sound of another car skidding, followed by breaking glass. "Three of the drivers below," he corrected. But that count was followed by another loud crunch and more screeching brakes. "Literally many of the drivers below are being distracted by our extremely dazzling sign," he admitted finally.

"Quick! Turn it off!" Freddie yelled.

Carly started to panic. "Hurry!"

Spencer was totally panicking, too. "I will now turn off the sign," he said. He worked the remote control and the sign started blinking super fast. That was even worse. It sounded as if every car on the highway was banging into every other car.

"That's not off!" Freddie yelled.

Carly screamed. "Spencer!"

Spencer was frantically working the remote control. "Oh man," he moaned. "I'm pushing the buttons. Literally all of them, trying to turn off the sign."

"You're going to overload the circuits!" Freddie warned.

The sign started to spark and pop. The letters began to flicker and then some of them burned out. Finally it stopped blinking, and went dark for a moment. When it came back on the remaining letters read:

"Pee on Carl?" Sam asked.

"Turn that off!" Carly insisted.

Spencer was still frantically working the remote control, but he was distracted by everything going on around him. "I'm trying! If the stupid cars would just —" He stopped and yelled down at the passing cars. "Don't look at the sign! Stop beholding the sign!"

Carly heard another crunch, but it was quieter this time.

Spencer looked at his feet. "Awww, I stepped on my taco," he said.

And with that, somehow, the sign finally went out. The sound of cars crashing was replaced by the sound of police sirens.

Chapter 6

A couple of hours later, Carly, Sam, and Freddie were checking their viewer email on the computer in the kitchen. Their audience loved their contest!

"Wait, wait, and read this one," Sam said.

Carly and Freddie read over her shoulder.

"Insane," Carly said.

Freddie shook his head. "Unbelievable."

"I know, can you believe this?" Sam asked.

"Duh," Freddie told her. "I said unbelievable."

"Oh, I'm sorry," Sam said. "I thought you said you were annoying."

"All right," Freddie warned her. "One more comment like that —"

Carly was about to grab her spray bottle, but Freddie's threat was cut off by the doorbell.

"Try not to hurt each other while I get the door," Carly told them.

She opened it to find Spencer in handcuffs. There were police officers on either side of him. Sheepishly, Spencer raised his hands and waved at Carly.

"Does he belong to you?" one of the officers asked.

"Yes, sir," she answered. "He's my brother."

Sam and Freddie walked over to check out what was going on. They watched the police officer unlock Spencer's handcuffs.

"Thank you, officer," Spencer said, rubbing his wrists. "Do you have any lotion?"

"No!" the officer barked. "Now I'm letting you off with a warning. But next time you cause one of the worst traffic jams in Seattle history, you will get arrested."

Carly nodded. "I think that sounds fair."

"What were you thinking?" the officer asked Spencer. "Putting up a sign telling people to pee on Carl."

"It was a terrible mistake, Officer . . ." Spencer paused to read the officer's name tag. ". . . Carl."

Officer Carl glared at Spencer one last time before leaving.

Carly and Spencer quickly closed the door. Spencer was relieved to be home and handcuff-free. Carly was just happy to have him back.

Spencer sighed. "Well, that was —"

The doorbell rang again, and Spencer opened the door to find that Officer Carl was back. "And just so you know," Officer Carl said, pulling a small plastic bottle out of his pocket, "I did have lotion." He squirted some onto his hands and rubbed it in. "Cucumber melon," he said, giving his hands a sniff.

He left again. Spencer closed the door and locked it this time. "That was weird."

"Yeah," Freddie said.

"Way weird," Sam agreed.

"Anyway, sorry I kind of ruined your Webcast tonight," Spencer said.

"You didn't!" Freddie told him.

"C'mere," Sam said, pulling him toward the computer.

Spencer was totally confused. "What?"

"We were just reading the comment boards," Carly explained, working the mouse. "Listen to this one. 'The spaghetti in the blender made me

12

LOL. But I swear, when your brother's sign said 'Pee on Carl' . . ."

"Now read the one below it, about *Seattle Beat*," Sam urged her.

"Oh yeah, here." Carly scrolled down. "'Carly, loved seeing you and Sam on *Seattle Beat*. Sorry about the wet banner, but that was hilarious. I'm going to forward that clip to every kid in my school. Rock on, *iCarly*!'"

Spencer was totally impressed. "*Sweeeet*. How many comments like that?" he asked.

"Tons," Sam told him.

"People are linking to us," Freddie said.

"Telling their friends," Sam added.

"Okay, so wait," Spencer said, figuring it all out. "We all failed miserably trying to get you more viewers for *iCarly*."

Freddie nodded.

"Uh-huh," Sam agreed.

"And yet it is precisely those miserable failures that are getting you more viewers for *iCarly*," Spencer continued.

"Yep!" Sam told him.

Freddie nodded again. "Right."

"Insanity!" Spencer exclaimed.

"Oh, hey, we almost forgot the best part," Carly said.

"Yeah?" Sam asked.

Carly grinned. "Since all of us pretty much lost the contest, none of us have to touch Lewbert's wart!"

"That's right," Freddie said, remembering.

That called for a celebration.

"Well, then I say: Let's go get us some low-fat, cheeseless vegetarian pizza!" Spencer said.

They all cheered as they headed for the door.

Carly noticed her brother's chafed wrists and thought of one more thing they might need to make their celebration complete.

"And some cucumber melon lotion?" she asked.

"Please!" Spencer agreed.

Carly laughed. Maybe Spencer almost got arrested. Maybe she and Sam got drenched at *Seattle Beat*. But their audience thought they were great.

iCarly was a hit!